Mail Order Bride:
The Bride's Unexpected Baby

By
Faith Johnson

Clean and Wholesome Western
Historical Romance

Copyright © 2022 by Faith Johnson

All rights reserved.
No part of this book may be reproduced,
stored in a retrieval system, or
transmitted in any form, or by any
means, electronic, mechanical,
photocopying, recording or otherwise,
without prior permission of the author
or publisher.

Printed in the United States of America

Table of Contents

Unsolicited Testimonials............... 4

FREE GIFT............................. 5

Chapter One 6

Chapter Two 19

Chapter Three 30

Chapter Four 47

Chapter Five 56

Chapter Six........................... 73

Chapter Seven 88

Chapter Eight 101

Epilogue 107

FREE GIFT............................ 111

Please Check out My Other Works..... 112

Thank You............................ 113

Unsolicited Testimonials

By **Glaidene Ramsey**
⭐⭐⭐⭐⭐ I so enjoy reading Faith Johnson's stories. This Bride and groom met as she arrived in town. They were married and then the story begins.!!!! Enjoy

By **Voracious Reader**
⭐⭐⭐⭐⭐ "Great story of love and of faith. The hardships we may have to go through and how with faith, and God's help we can get through them" -

By **Glaidene's reads**
⭐⭐⭐⭐⭐ "Faith Johnson is a five star writer. I have read a majority of her books. I enjoyed the story and hope you will too!!!!!"

By **Kirk Statler**
⭐⭐⭐⭐⭐ I liked the book. A different twist because she wasn't in contract with anyone when she went. She went. God provided for her needs. God blessed her above and beyond.

By **Amazon Customer**
⭐⭐⭐⭐⭐ Great clean and easy reading, a lot of fun for you to know ignores words this is crazy so I'll not reviewing again. Let me tell it and go

By **Kindle Customer**
⭐⭐⭐⭐⭐ Wonderful story. You have such a way of showing people that opposite do attack. Both in words and action. I am glad that I found your books.

Just to say thanks for checking our works we like to gift you

Our Exclusive Never Before Released Books

100% FREE!

Please GO TO

http://cleanromancepublishing.com/gift

And get your FREE gift

Thanks for being such a wonderful client.

Chapter One

"Are you sure that you really want to do this?" Kevin asked his sister Amanda. A loud whistle sounded beside them, causing them to both tense up and shield their ears for a moment. As they waited for the sound to dissipate, they both eyed the snow flurries that fell on them.

"Of course I do," Amanda said with a smile and a shrug, her voice fogging up the air. "Why wouldn't I want to?"

Kevin sighed and began to list the items, ticking them off one finger at a time. "You will be leaving me. You don't even know the man... in fact, you don't know anyone there. And well, you might not see me again."

Amanda smiled at him and touched his arm. "I think it sounds like you will miss me."

Kevin pouted. "Well, yes, and all the other things too."

Amanda held out her hand and began to tick off her own fingers. "You have your lovely wife to keep you company, Mom and Dad are gone and won't miss me, Dr. Steven James is waiting on and wanting me to be his wife, I will get to live in a new place in the West, experiencing new things, I will get to find love, and I will get to have a career as a nurse alongside my new husband."

She held up both her hands triumphantly. "I have more reasons to go than you have reasons for me to stay. Besides, you both can always come and visit me. Take a little vacation away from the East coast."

Kevin sighed, his face turning sour because he knew that his sister was right. Then, the train began to whistle again. As it did, Amanda pulled Kevin forward and into a large hug. When the loud sound was gone, they released. "I will miss you," Kevin said.

"I will miss you too," Amanda confirmed. "I promise I will write to you as soon as I get there. You will only read about how wonderful my life is," she smiled brightly at him, and he stuck his tongue out at her. After another quick hug, Amanda picked up her suitcase, made sure that she had her ticket ready, and headed over to the train, ready to start her new life.

After getting her ticket checked and her luggage put up, she quickly sat down and looked out the window. After just a moment, she found her brother in the small crowd. They waved as the train began to take off, lurching to a start, the wheels squeaking and the engine pounding. Within a moment, Kevin and the train station were just small specks in the distance. The farther away from them that Amanda went, the more her heart thudded with excitement and a little bit of worry.

Of course, it was quite natural to worry at least a little bit. The only way she consoled herself was to think about the wonderful new love that she was headed to, this lovely doctor who would be waiting for her.

***

The hours seemed to pass by slowly, dragging on longer than Amanda had expected. She knew that it was a far journey, but she never expected her back to hurt so much or her legs to ache from not being used. There were not many other passengers on the train, although they did pick up some people along the way. But it seemed that the further they got, the more people got off the train at different stops. Slowly, the train was emptying out.

Amanda looked out the window, watching the snowy landscape pass with both excitement and calm. Although she found the landscape fascinating and unlike anything else she had seen before, she also found it to be very redundant. Soon enough, she was able to drift off to sleep, the continuing landscape being the image that played in her mind as she rested.

Throughout the next few stops, when the train would lurch to a halt, Amanda would wake up in a panic. Looking around and identifying what station they had stopped at would set her mind at ease and allow her to drift back to sleep a little longer. Finally, after the fourth stop and panicked awakening, Amanda resolved to just stay awake and not be surprised. To keep herself aware, she daydreamed about what her life would be like as she worked side-by-side with her new husband. Her excitement warmed her heart greatly.

Finally, Amanda's station was coming up. As soon as she realized it, she could hardly keep still. She tapped her foot on the ground and fiddled with her fingers, wishing that the train would stop so that she could gather her luggage. As soon as the locomotive puffed to halt, she was the first one out the door without a moment of hesitation. She stepped out the door only to fall into a large drift of snow.

"Ahh," she muttered, pulling herself out of the snow. "Cold, cold, cold," she said, her teeth chattering as she walked towards the closest buildings.

Steve had explained in his last letter that his office was within a short walk from the train station and that she was to meet him there. Following the streets and directions that Steven had sent, Amanda easily made it through the snow and to the little doctor's office just off the main road. As she approached it, she noticed its quaint appearance and tidy signs. A lantern was lit inside, the light shining through the windows and lighting up the door.

Amanda quickly entered, pulling the door shut as fast as she could. A bell attached to the door rang feverishly at her quick movements. Straight ahead was a desk, but no one was sitting there. Indeed, the room was quite empty. Where could Steven be?

Hesitantly, Amanda walked up to the desk. Once she reached it, she saw instructions on the countertop indicating that she should ring the additional bell beside the instructions for assistance. Picking the small handbell up carefully, she gave it a few swings, releasing the sound of chimes into the air.

"I'll be right with you," called a man's voice. Upon hearing him, Amanda's face at once broke out into a smile. That had to be her future husband. She stood anxiously, waiting for him to come out and greet her. As she did, a small cry broke into her thoughts.

Looking past the counter, she stood up on her tiptoes to see a long hallway with a few different doors going down it. All the doors were closed. However, behind the counter where a worker would stand was a makeshift crib with a tiny new baby bundled up inside it.

Ohh, Steven must be with a client who has a child. That's why he isn't at the counter. The baby moved its balled-up fists, tossing them in the air. Amanda watched it with a slight amount of apprehension. She never had been very comfortable around small children.

After a moment, one of the doors opened, and a lovely woman stepped out. She stopped just outside the door and looked inside. "Thank you so much, Doctor. Will we be seeing you in church this Sunday?"

Dr. James let out a laugh that lit up the room. "If I am free and available, then of course."

The woman chuckled slightly and released a small giggle, her cheeks turning slightly pink. Amanda frowned at the sight. But then the woman turned away from Steven and walked around and counter, past Amanda, and out the door. The bell rang behind her.

"Oh, wait... you forgot your baby," Amanda said as the door latched shut.

Steven let out a chuckle, coming out from the room to see Amanda. "Do you mean this baby?" Amanda turned to see that he was indeed pointing at the one behind the counter.

"Yes," Amanda said with hesitation. Was there another baby?

"That's not her baby," he told her. "Can I help you?"

"Oh, I'm Amanda. I've just come from the train station."

"Amanda," he exclaimed with a large smile. "It is so nice to meet you. Sorry that you had to walk over here all by yourself."

"It wasn't a problem," Amanda told him as she mentally noted her very wet boots. She might have to get better ones if she was always going to be walking through the snow. She looked carefully at her husband-to-be. He was dressed neatly in a long white coat over a button-down shirt and nice trousers. His blonde hair hung slightly over his forehead in a casual way, and his green eyes seemed to sparkle every time his dimple came out when he smiled.

The baby started crying in large wails of anger, its fists bundled up and its face turning red. Steven immediately bent down, his face full of concern. Then, he swooped the child up in an easy action and began to cradle it in his arms.

"There, there," he said gently. The baby slowly began to settle until it was finally just looking up at him. Steven smiled slightly, but there was a pain in his expression. A guilt or a sadness, Amanda was not sure.

Steven looked up at Amanda. "Unfortunately, since we last communicated, things have changed."

Chapter Two

Amanda's heart began to pound with fear. Did he no longer want to marry her?

"This is my sister's child," he said plainly. He looked at the baby, his face still full of sadness.

"Oh, you're an uncle, that's wonderful," Amanda said, gathering all the excitement she could.

Steven smiled at her, a soft but sad smile. When he started speaking again, his voice was even quieter than it had been before, and his smile was gone. "My sister died in childbirth."

Amanda stood, frozen for a moment, absorbing the information. "And the father?"

Steven released a sigh. "He ran off as soon as he heard that she was dead. I'm the only family that this little girl has left."

Amanda was shocked. She did not expect this at all.

Steven continued to look at her until the baby started to cry in large, fitful sounds. Steven cuddled her closer, turning and slowly bouncing her up and down.

"There there," he told her in a hushed voice. He continued to bounce the baby as he moved towards the back of the building and disappeared around the corner. Amanda watched him go, unsure if she should be following or not.

After a little bit of time had passed, Amanda was uncertain if Steven would come back. How had this happened? Suddenly there was a child that she and her soon-to-be husband would have to take care of, and it wasn't even theirs.

"Steven?" Amanda called out hesitantly. She waited, listening, but no sound came. With a sigh, she slowly stepped behind the counter, following where Steven had disappeared to. As she reached one of the rooms, she paused and glanced inside the slightly open door. Inside the dark room was a small patient table, a desk with supplies on it, and a few chairs. The supplies were a mixture of bandages, rags, vials of liquid, and other items.

Moving past the room, Amanda glanced in the next three doors that she passed. Each was the same as the first, as all of them seemed to be rooms for patients. When Amanda reached the end of the room, she found a staircase leading upstairs.

Approaching the wooden stairs, she touched the handrail lightly and looked up, trying to see where they led. "Steven?" she called again.

"Come on up," came a faint cry from upstairs. With a frown, Amanda began to climb the stairs. Soon enough, she had reached the landing. Stepping in, she found herself in a whole little home on the second floor. Just ahead, she could see a kitchen and a sitting room with doors that led off to other rooms. The noise was coming from the kitchen, so Amanda continued towards it. As she rounded the corner, she found Steven standing with the baby in his arms, a bottle perched up in his hand as he fed the baby.

Steven looked up as she approached. "Hello," he said softly with a large smile. Amanda's heart jumped when he looked at her like that. "Once again, I'm sorry for not meeting you at the station. I just have to be at the office most of the day for clients. Although sometimes I do have to leave it for home visits. So, how was the train ride? Hopefully, there were no problems."

Amanda shrugged. "It was fine. Nothing really to note. So, are you really keeping the baby?" The question was out before she could stop herself.

Steven frowned. "She has no one else. I can't abandon her."

Holding up her hands, Amanda quickly explained. "That's not what I was meaning... Just, won't it be hard to run your practice with a baby."

"It would be," Steven agreed. "except that now you're here. So you'll be able to help out a lot."

"Well," Amanda hesitated. "I was just hoping to help out with your practice."

"You will," Steven said in a very reassuring manner. His eyes left her to look down at the baby. Amanda noticed that he watched her as if she were a glass figurine that would break if he looked too hard.

"I was thinking of naming her Joyce," he said out loud, although Amanda wondered if he was actually talking to her or not.

"That's very lovely," she replied after a minute of silence. He continued to stare at the little baby girl until he looked up at Amanda.

"That was her mother's name."

Amanda didn't say anything. Steven turned away from her, still holding the baby. He rocked her gently as he paced around the kitchen. "Is tomorrow a good time for the marriage ceremony? I already have it all arranged with the Reverend." He spoke while facing away from her, his voice coming out slightly muffled.

"That's fine," Amanda answered, relieved to be talking about something else. Steven nodded, his back still facing her. "Is there anything I can help with tonight before it is time to go to sleep?" she asked.

Steven's pacing paused slightly as he thought. He then turned to her. "Would you-uh-could you wash some of the cloth diapers? We are running low." His cheeks turned pink as he spoke.

Amanda stood there for just a moment. But before the shock could set in, she began to nod her head. After all, she was here to help, right?

"I can do that. Where are they?"

Steven motioned his head towards the door at the left of the hallway. Amanda turned and walked towards it, quickly opening the door and peeking inside. It seemed to be Steven's room. The bed was very messy, the blankets all strewn and rumpled. A lovely cradle sat just to the side of his bed, and beside it was a large pile of used diapers.

Taking a deep breath, Amanda quickly gathered up the diapers and made her way to the sink in the kitchen, where she placed them in a pile on the counter. After Steven directed her, she took a large pail and gathered some well water from their collection bucket downstairs. Lugging the heavy container back up the stairs, she placed it on the stove and began to heat the water. As she waited for it to get warmer, she walked back down the stairs to collect the bags she had left by the front door.

Once she had carried them back upstairs, she returned to the kitchen to ask Steven where to place them, but to her surprise, he was gone, and his bedroom door was shut.

She placed her bags in the sitting room and went back to the diapers with a sigh. Once the water was warm enough, she dumped them in and got to work scrubbing with the lye soap. Once everything had been cleaned, Amanda easily found the hanging lines by the fireplace, where she began to pin the diapers up. She only had a few up when the door to Steven's room opened and he exited quietly, carefully shutting the door behind himself. He walked over to her with a small smile.

"She's finally asleep."

Amanda attempted to return his smile with an equally happy one, but she was unsure if it worked. For a moment, they just stared at each other. Then, finally, Steven walked over and bent down beside her to begin pinning diapers up. Amanda was surprised by this, but she didn't say anything, happy to have the help and the company. Very quickly, they finished. It was then that Steven noticed her bags on the other side of the room.

"I'm sorry," he said. "I forgot to show you your room." He led her to the door on the right side of the hallway and opened it. "This is where you can sleep."

"Thank you," Amanda said with a nod. The room was modest with a simple bed and dresser, but it would do just fine. She placed her bags on the bed and turned around, looking at him. "Is there anything else you would like me to work on tonight?"

"Oh, no, I'm fine. I'm sure you've had a long day and you would like to rest," Steven replied.

Even though Amanda was willing to stay up, she was grateful for his words. Soon she was in her own room, the door shut. After removing her uncomfortable clothes, she sank into bed and almost instantly fell asleep.

Chapter Three

Steven watched Amanda disappear into her room. As she left, he felt a pang of emotion in his chest, although he wasn't sure what it meant. Even though he could no longer see her, he thought about her and their interactions that day. She had lovely dark hair that was paired with golden-brown eyes. The colors went very well together. Her simple winter dress wasn't warm enough for winters in the West, but it was neat and efficient. Even so, he would have to take her to the seamstress to get her something more appropriate for the next few months.

Steven was curious about Amanda, though he knew her a bit from their letters. She seemed intelligent and willing, but he wasn't sure how much time she would need to start adapting to living with him in their home. He knew he had surprised her with the baby, but he truly had not meant to, and he'd had no other choice.

With a sigh, he moved towards the kitchen and began to tidy up. He thought of his sister as he did so, and how much he missed her at this moment. They had always been close, and he still was not quite over her sudden death. He had never really cared for his sister's husband, he mused, but he had certainly not expected the man to run out on her.

It was then that he began to hear Joyce crying. He waited a moment in perfect silence to see if Joyce would fall back asleep on her own. When the baby didn't settle down and her cries began to increase, he quickly jogged up the stairs, making his way to the room. He noticed that Amanda's door hadn't moved for her to check on the baby or to see if he would attend to the baby. Perhaps she was a deep sleeper?

Entering the room, he quickly picked up Joyce and began to rock her once again in a soft, swaying motion. Almost immediately, she was comforted back to sleep. With a sigh of relief, he slowed his motion and began to lean back over the bar of the crib to lower her inside. At the sudden drop, Joyce began to cry and wiggle again, desperate for him to not put her down. Steven let out a groan and lifted her back up and into his arms once more. He made his way over to the bed, where he sat down and waited for her to fall into a deeper sleep.

The rest of the night progressed similarly. Joyce would sleep fitfully for only small amounts of time between diapers changes and feedings. Steven felt like he was losing his mind by the time that dawn began to approach and the baby finally fell into a deeper sleep.

Steven carefully crept out of the room, closing the door gently behind him. With still no sound of Joyce having woken up, he moved to the sitting room, where he fell onto the couch in exhaustion. Almost instantly, he felt a wave of sleepiness taking him. As his eyelids fluttered shut, he promised himself that it would just be for a moment. Just a moment of sleep.

***

Amanda woke up to the sun peeking through her window. She sat up in a frantic state, not quite sure where she was. After a moment, though, she remembered the day before and her journey across the states.

Getting up, she padded across the room in just her nightgown, her feet bare and cold. Reaching the window, which was covered in long curtains, she pulled part of the fabric back, peeking through to see outside. Her room had a lovely view over the entire street. She saw that a few of the windows of other buildings were starting to be lit with light from people stirring and getting ready for their days. However, outside on the snowy street, there was no one that she could see, though there were some tracks and footprints.

She shivered from the cold draft coming through the window frame and quickly put the curtain back. Walking over to her suitcase, she began to dig through it until she found the nicest dress that she had packed. It wasn't white, and the trim and lace weren't new, but it would have to do. After fixing her hair and getting dressed, she opened her bedroom door and peeked out, first looking towards Steven's door.

It was closed. She listened but didn't notice any obvious sounds. Frowning, she stepped out into the hallway and closed her own door. Heading towards the kitchen, she blinked in surprise to see Steven asleep on the couch. For a moment, she stood, frozen. Her eyes lingered on him, wondering what she should do. She knew that he would most likely be upset with her staring, but she found that she couldn't help herself. This man was going to be her husband. And so far, everything had lived up to what she had hoped, except for the baby.

Where was the baby, anyway?

With a shake of her head, she moved on to the kitchen. Searching the cupboards, she found some food to make and quickly got to work, heating up the stove and getting out cooking utensils. When she had a nice mixture of grits and eggs ready, she plated up the food and placed it on the table.

Stepping out of the kitchen, Amanda looked over at Steven, who was still fast asleep. For a moment, she debated on what to do, to wake him or not. Finally, she decided that he could use the sleep. So with a shrug, she went ahead and ate her food before cleaning up from the meal.

Just as she was finishing putting away the newly washed dishes, cries of the baby sounded throughout the home. Steven sat up with a jump, causing a large crash of sound as he hit the floor hard with his feet. Amanda heard him quickly head back to his room, the door closing behind him. After only a short time, he appeared from the bedroom, baby in his arms, heading for the kitchen.

"Oh," he said when he nearly ran into Amanda. He looked at her with confusion before finally shaking his head and moving around her. He quickly began to prepare some milk. "I didn't realize that you were in here," he said, his voice slightly raspy from a lack of sleep.

Amanda shrugged, unsure, and said. "I made breakfast," as she pointed towards the table. Steven turned, bottle in hand, to look at the food.

"Thank you," he said, a smile coming to his face as he turned back to look at her. Then he noticed her outfit, his eyes scanning up and down her. "You look nice," he said before the realization hit him and his face paled slightly. "We're getting married today."

Amanda tilted her head. "You definitely don't sound very excited," she said, with a smile to soften her joke.

Steven shook his head quickly, the bottle now in the baby's mouth. "That's not what I meant… I just forgot that we were doing that first thing this morning. I guess I got carried away with everything…"

Still holding the baby, he disappeared down the hall and into his room. After a little bit, he reappeared with the baby, both now fully dressed and ready to go. Steven had changed into a nice outfit with freshly pressed pants and a neat blazer. The baby was swaddled in multiple layers, prepared to go outside.

The group made their way downstairs, where Steven had them wait at the back door of the building. After passing Joyce off to Amanda, Steven disappeared outside.

Amanda waited rather impatiently, doing her best to not be bothered by the child. After a moment, she glanced down at the bundle in her arms and couldn't help but smile at the large eyes that were looking back up at her. The child's eyes were a brilliant green that seemed to shimmer in the right light. Amanda found herself getting lost in them until she heard the carriage pull up outside the door.

And just like that, Amanda had hardened herself against the infant once more, not quite ready to like it yet. Though she knew it was not the baby's fault, Amanda was still a bit angry with how things had turned out so far. How could she be both a nurse and mother to this child?

Steven soon appeared at the door and quickly hustled them to the covered wagon. As soon as Amanda and Joyce were situated, Steven climbed onto the front of the wagon and used the reins to start the horse moving forward. After only a short trip across town, they finally reached the church, where Steven pulled the horse to a stop near the front door. Quickly getting down, Steven helped Amanda out, making sure that Joyce was firmly in her arms before he climbed back onto the wagon and drove it over to the hitching post.

Amanda quickly walked inside, the baby pressed against her chest to keep away the cold wind and air. As the door closed behind her, a voice greeted her.

"Good morning. Are you here with Dr. James?"

Amanda turned to see an older gentleman dressed very nicely, a Bible in his hands.

She nodded. "Yes, he is putting the wagon away now." The man nodded in return before turning his attention to the bundle in her arms.

Reaching out, he moved the blanket away from Joyce's face, a sad smile on his own. "It's such a tragic shame," he gently said with a shake of his head. Amanda nodded in agreement, uncertain of what to say.

Thankfully, she didn't have to. The door burst open as Steven hurried in, pushing the door shut behind him and closing out the cold air. "Hello, Reverend Marcus. Sorry that we are running late," Steven greeted.

The Reverend waved his hand with a shake of his head. "Not a problem at all. Let's get you two married, shall we?"

Reverend Marcus led them to a small, personal room. Inside were a few sets of tables and chairs. He had them sit down at one of the tables, where he began his speech about their marriage under God. He spoke of taking care of your partner and supporting them, being there for each other when no one else could be. Finally, he got to their vows. Within seconds, both of them had said, 'I do.' Marcus clapped his hands in congratulations, and Steven leaned over and quickly kissed Amanda's cheek, making her blush.

After they signed their names, Marcus scooped up the documents. "I will file these, and you will be able to pick up your license soon." He stood up from the table and held out his hand for Steven to shake. "If you two will excuse me, I have some other business to attend to." With that, he left the newly wedded couple, the room becoming suddenly quite silent. Steven and Amanda sat for a moment, taking in this new change.

Suddenly, Joyce began to get fidgety in Amanda's arms. She did her best to hold onto the baby, but she wiggled with great strength. Steven helped get the baby resituated before standing up. "We'd better head back to the office. I have a few house calls that I need to make today."

"Really?" Amanda asked, excitement entering her voice. "That sounds like fun." She stood up and readjusted the baby in her arms.

Steven frowned. "There are a few families who have some very sick members. I will be delivering medicine to them and checking on them. We don't want them coming into town on their own and getting worse."

"Of course," Amanda agreed, becoming more somber, but the excitement still remained in her chest.

"That is one reason I'm very glad that you're here. Otherwise, I'm not sure what I would have done with Joyce." Steven ushered them out of the room as he spoke, closing the door behind them.

"What do you mean?" Amanda asked, confused. "Am I, er, are we not coming with you?"

"Oh no," Steven said, his eyes growing slightly wide. "You might be able to handle being around sick people, but a new baby needs to stay as healthy as possible. So you two will need to stay at the office."

He looked over at Amanda to find that her expression had become much sadder. "What's wrong?" he asked.

"Nothing really," Amanda answered quickly. "I was just hoping that I could help you today."

Steven smiled kindly at her answer. "You will be helping me today. Watching

Joyce is a great help. Besides, you can help manage the office while I am gone. Some folks come by occasionally just for supplies."

Amanda nodded her head in an attempt to seem all right with the situation. After reaching the door to the church, Amanda once more waited while holding Joyce as Steven fetched the wagon. *Would that be her life,* she wondered, *forever holding this child and waiting?*

Chapter Four

Soon they were back home. After the buggy had stopped, Amanda quickly got out. She carried the baby inside, heading up to the second floor. Once she got there, Steven showed her where all the supplies were and how he had been changing the diapers and giving the bottles. He figured that Amanda already had experience but might need a refresher. As soon as he felt confident in her abilities, he changed his clothes, grabbed his medical bag and a crate of medicine and then was off, heading out in the wagon.

As soon as he was gone, Amanda felt lost. It had been a while since she had taken care of a baby, and that had just been one day with a friend. After trying to put her into her crib, Amanda found that Joyce preferred to be held. But with a bit of persuasion of the bottle, she was able to lay her down as soon as the baby's stomach was full and empty of bubbles.

Leaving the room and closing the door behind her, Amanda released a sigh of relief when Joyce didn't start crying. Then, carefully creeping over to the kitchen, Amanda made some lunch for herself. She walked around the small home as she ate her sandwich, looking at the different decorations and furniture items. She noticed that everything was of excellent quality. Although the house was not large and there wasn't much to it, it was all very tidy and clearly well cared for.

While Amanda found it encouraging that Steven was able to clean up after himself, she also felt a little disappointed, knowing that he would expect the same from her. She began to clean with a small sigh, all while listening carefully for a small cry to let her know that she was needed elsewhere.

The day passed this way. Amanda would shift between taking care of Joyce and cleaning the home. Eventually, she moved them both downstairs, placing Joyce in her crib on the first floor. However, every area in the office was already free from any dust or dirt. Clearly, Steven took care of this area very well—it was even cleaner than the house.

Just as Amanda was considering bringing Joyce back upstairs, the door pushed open, the bell ringing wildly as a woman walked in.

"Hello, how can I help you?" Amanda asked with excitement as soon as the door was shut. The woman looked up in surprise, obviously not expecting to see Amanda.

"Who are you?" the woman asked as she stepped closer to the counter.

"I'm Amanda," Amanda introduced herself. "Dr. James and I have just been married. He is out at the moment. What can I help you with?"

The woman's face turned to disgust. "Dr. James, married? I have not heard a word of this, and I hear everything." She lifted an eyebrow up, staring down Amanda.

"What can I help you with, Miss…?" Amanda asked, trying to ignore the woman's comment.

"It's Mrs.," she snarled. Then, lifting up her nose, she continued. "Mrs. Helen

Baker. My husband and I were out running errands. I always come by to visit Dr. James on days such as this. That poor man is always so lonely and in need of company.”

Amanda ground her teeth together, trying to ignore the new pain in her heart. “I’m sorry, Mrs. Baker, but this is a doctor’s office. Please only come back if you are in need of his professional services.”

Helen narrowed her eyes and then turned, swiftly leaving the building, the door slamming shut behind her. As soon as she was gone, Amanda’s shoulders slumped. What a horrible woman. She hurried to the door and locked it, flipping the sign to ‘closed.’ Then she picked up Joyce and went back upstairs.

As evening came, Amanda found herself getting more and more impatient, wondering when Steven would return. When the sky grew dark, she finally gave up and began to place Joyce to bed in her crib. Worried that she wouldn't be able to hear the baby if she cried, Amanda sat outside the door, propping her head up with her arm and slowly fading off to sleep.

She woke with a startle at the feeling of a hand touching her shoulder. Jumping, she quickly began to look around. "It's alright, it's just me," said a voice. Amanda looked to find Steven.

"Oh, you're home," she mumbled, slowly pulling herself up. Steven helped her the rest of the way to her feet. "I'm heading to bed," Amanda told him with a yawn before turning and going to her room. As soon as the door was closed behind her, she fell into the bed, fully clothed, pulled the blankets over her and fell asleep.

***

The next few weeks passed like this. On the days that Steven was home, he would be downstairs at the office, taking care of clients. Amanda would be stuck upstairs, tending to the baby and the cooking and cleaning. Most days, she could just hear the voices of the conversations below, as Steven would go about his day, not even knowing just how much Amanda wished that she was down there too.

For the most part, she became accepting of the baby, dealing with the diapers and cleaning that came with Joyce. But sometimes, at the dinner table, Steven would share an excited recount of all he had done for his patients that day, and Amanda would feel her resentment for Joyce start to grow ever slightly. Finally, after Steven finished dinner, he would take over with Joyce, getting her to bed and allowing Amanda some freedom to sit in her room, looking out the window or working on some sewing alone.

Her slim amount of happiness came from the letters she would write to her brother, Kevin. She did not even wait for a response to her letters before she wrote him again. Unfortunately, the mail was terribly slow, and she could not bear it. And so, every evening she had the energy, she wrote to him, telling him all about her new life. He would receive many letters from her at some point, but for now, all she could do was wait and write to him.

The house began to grow less organized throughout the days, less clean. Amanda did her best to keep up with it, but she found it terribly difficult. She was pleased every evening that Steven didn't mention the mess.

But out of all the days, the ones when Steven did his house calls were the hardest on Amanda. Those days, there were no other sounds of adult humans, no life around her. It was just her and the baby.

Amanda could feel herself fading with each one of these days as she waited patiently for her husband to get home.

Chapter Five

Steven stepped wearily off of the wagon and walked his horse the rest of the way into the barn. After unhitching it, he walked it to its stable, and then after checking its food and water, he headed to his home, happy that the day was over.

Unlocking the back door, he closed it and began to walk up the stairs as quietly as possible, hoping not to disturb Amanda and Joyce. When he got to the upper floor, he noticed that Amanda was not outside the room as usual. Carefully, he lowered his bag and walked farther into the home, looking around.

It was then that he noticed her sitting at the table, her head in her hands. He paused and watched her, trying to determine if she was only tired or if there was something else wrong. And as he did so, small details began to catch his attention. The first weeks she had lived with him, her hair had always been neatly done up in braids or twists. But tonight, it was loose and frizzy, and it looked like it had been that way for a while. A stack of dirty dishes and dirty rags was on the table with her. The kitchen counters were also full of food items and other dirty utensils. Nothing was in its place or put away.

Upon noticing this, sadness and frustration took over him. How had he not seen it before? He was a doctor, for crying out loud. He took a deep breath to calm himself and then slowly walked over to her. Hearing him approach, Amanda looked up, lifting up her face. Steven noticed the dark circles under her eyes and the paleness to her skin that hadn't always been there. Clearly, she was exhausted—and he had not noticed.

"I'm sorry," Amanda said, wiping her face. "I didn't hear you come in."

Steven sat down beside her without saying a word and gently took her hand into his own. He stared into her brown eyes for a long moment, wishing that he had done better.

Amanda tilted her head. "Is something wrong?"

The corner of Steven's mouth moved as he nodded his head. "I have failed you."

Amanda blinked in surprise, a fear entering her eyes. "What do you mean? Is it that Baker woman?"

Steven frowned. "I'm not sure what you mean…What I meant to say was that I'm sorry for what I have put you through."

"I don't understand," Amanda said, standing up quickly. "Do you not want me here anymore? Do you want me to go?"

"Oh no," he cooed, standing up with her. He gently pulled her into a hug, his arms wrapping around her in a warm embrace. "That's not what I mean at all," he whispered.

After embracing for a moment, Amanda pulled away enough to look at him. "What do you mean?" She was tired, and his words were not making sense to her.

"It's all been too much. I've given you too much to do," Steven explained. "The baby, the cleaning, the cooking. It's too much to put on you." Amanda's shoulders sagged at his explanation. He held her for a little while longer. "What can I do to help you?"

Amanda was quiet for a moment before she looked up at him. "I would really love it if you could take care of Joyce in the evenings, once you are done working, of course."

Steven frowned. "Don't I already do that?"

Stepping back from him, she held her hands out to explain. "What I mean is, instead of you staying downstairs to clean everything up, come up here to watch Joyce, and I'll clean up down there."

"Are you sure that won't just be more work?"

"It will be a nice change of pace and scenery. And this way, you will be able to spend more time with her," Amanda explained.

Steven shook his head, not quite understanding, but then he shrugged his shoulders. "If that will help you, then that sounds like a good plan to me."

"Thank you so much," she said with new energy as she wrapped her arms around him once more. Suddenly, they both realized that this was the first time they had truly hugged. Breaking apart awkwardly, they smiled at each other in a shy way.

"If you want to head to bed, that's fine," Steven finally said, breaking through the tension in the air. "I'm probably going to stay up for a bit to get some cleaning done. That should make things easier for us tomorrow."

Amanda thought for a moment. "How about we clean up together?"

After agreeing, they both spent the evening talking and cleaning, with only small breaks for Steven to go into his room and soothe Joyce back to sleep. They discussed their lives before each other. Amanda's dead parents and the brother she had left and missed so dearly. How she wanted something different, and that's why she'd answered his ad.

Steven discussed his lack of family and the loss of his sister. How everyone in town seemed to view him in such high esteem, and how they would never consider him human with flaws. How he had longed to find a wife, but the women in town seemed more interested in his prestige than actual company.

The hours rolled by faster than Amanda thought they would, and soon, they were headed to sleep with a slightly cleaner home and much happier hearts.

***

The next day, Amanda felt a new excitement as she went about her daily tasks taking care of Joyce and tending to their home. Steven was in his office today, so the sounds of people moving about were drifting up through the floorboards. Amanda was surprised to find that everything seemed much more bearable and not nearly as bad as it had the night before, now that Steven had spoken with her and helped her clean. Their interaction had given her world a new light.

As the day began to draw to a close, Amanda realized, with a start, that she would need to have dinner on the verge of being done before Steven came upstairs to take over. She rushed to the kitchen, baby in her arms, and tried to figure out what she could quickly make in order to be done before he climbed up the stairs. They needed to go to the general store and food market, so there were limited options, but Amanda decided on some potatoes and meat. After placing the baby on the floor on a blanket, she did her best, trying to quickly prepare everything. Working on skinning the potatoes, her fingers moved quickly as they maneuvered the blade all around.

"That smells good," Steven's voice from around the corner as he entered the kitchen, startling her. Amanda's hand slipped, and the blade skinned part of her knuckle. Gasping, she immediately dropped the knife into the sink and grasped her hand. Steven swooped forward, grabbing a glass of water.

"Hold out your hand," he told her. She did as he asked, and by doing so, got a good look at the blood that was pooling on her wound already. Steven dumped the water onto it, causing the cut to sting. Amanda winced but didn't say anything—after all, he was the doctor here. After carefully inspecting it, Steven went to get his briefcase of supplies that he kept in his room and brought it over. Shifting through his tools, he pulled out a small bandage and quickly wrapped up her finger to help with stopping the bleeding.

"Thank you," Amanda said, feeling pretty embarrassed.

"You're very welcome," Steven said as he gently lifted her wounded hand up and kissed the knuckle above the injured finger. Amanda attempted to hide her smile as her cheeks began to grow hot.

Suddenly, she glanced at the pot that she had on the stove. It still needed some more potatoes. "I'm sorry, I wasn't able to finish dinner before you came up here."

Steven frowned. "Why would you need to finish dinner?"

"Because that's my job," Amanda explained. "I wanted to have it done before I went downstairs to work."

Steven let out a gentle chuckle. "I am perfectly capable of finishing dinner. You don't have to do everything. Besides, you will be leaving to do more work. So it only makes sense that I would finish up the cooking."

Amanda smiled with relief, surprised at his response.

"Now go on," he said. "I've got this. I will see you in a little bit."

She nodded with a smile at him and then quickly stepped out of the kitchen, leaving the rest of it to him. As she was walking down the stairs, she heard the baby begin to cry. Pausing her step, she nearly turned around to help, but then remembered that taking care of the baby wasn't her job right now. With a large smile, she continued down the stairs.

As soon as she reached the bottom floor, she took a deep breath of relief. For a moment, she just wandered around, allowing herself to simply be. Once she felt content, she grabbed the cleaning supplies from one of the closets and then started at the front of the office.

As she cleaned, she thought about how much her life had changed already. Instead of working as a nurse like she had expected, she was instead a mother of sorts. Even so, she felt grateful for how things seemed to be working out. Steven was more eager to help than she would have anticipated, and she was thankful to him. And after all, here she was, working in a doctor's office on the western frontier. Well, cleaning a doctor's office—but that was a step, at least.

Finished with her tasks, she headed back up the stairs. As she climbed, she could smell dinner cooking. It smelled delicious, and it occurred to her as she walked that

Steven had only cooked for them a handful of times.

"Hello," he greeted as she walked in the door. "The food is done. We were just waiting for you." He was lying on the ground with Joyce, and he had a variety of toys spread out between them.

"Thank you," Amanda said. "Everything should be spotless in the office now. You'll have to let me know tomorrow if I missed anything."

"I'm sure that you didn't," Steven said with a shrug and smile. "That reminds me, I have a book from my school days that talks about how to treat a variety of ailments. Would you be interested in taking a look at it? I know previously you had said that you wanted to help out with the practice."

Amanda smiled brightly. "That would be just lovely. Thank you!"

The rest of the evening went smoothly. They ate dinner while sitting on the floor so that Joyce could keep playing. Steven would lean down and play with Joyce in between bites, moving a toy or tickling her feet. Amanda felt her heart warm watching the interaction. He was clearly a very loving man, and she couldn't help but smile as she watched them. Soon though, Joyce grew tired and began to fuss. Even though he hadn't finished his dinner yet, Steven swooped her up, and they went to make a bottle before disappearing into his room for a while.

While he was gone, Amanda worked on cleaning up from dinner. She was in the middle of dishes when he appeared in the kitchen, a very large and thick book in his hands. "This is the book I was telling you about. While I don't have everything memorized, you are welcome to keep it with you for the most part. I'll let you know if I ever need it," he said with a chuckle.

"Thank you so much," Amanda said. "I'm looking forward to reading it."

"Well, why don't you get started?" Steven offered.

"Oh, but the dishes—" Amanda began.

"I can handle the dishes," Steven told her.

For the rest of the evening, Amanda sat perched up on the couch as she read through the pages, her eyes scanning through all of the knowledge that was at her fingertips. Before she knew it, a few hours had passed and her eyes were stinging, her eyelids growing heavy. Leaving the book on the couch, she finally climbed into bed that night with her heart full and happy.

Chapter Six

The next day, Steven had been in his office for a few hours when he came upstairs unexpectedly. He found Amanda and Joyce in the sitting room, playing on the floor.

"I'm sorry, I forgot to tell you last night, but I have to make one house call today. It shouldn't take long, though. One of the ladies in town is going to be a new mother soon. I don't want her traveling in these snowy conditions, so I am going to go to her and see how she is doing. Then I will be right back. However, today is when the townsfolk expect me to be in office. Would you be able to stay downstairs and manage the office while I'm gone? I know that's a lot to ask for while you are watching Joyce."

Amanda only had to think for a moment before quickly nodding her head. "Of course. You go ahead. I will gather some supplies for her, and then we will be right down." Excitement fluttered in her belly, but she tried to keep her voice calm.

"Thank you so much," he said before coming over and giving them both a small hug. Then he stood up and headed back downstairs. Soon enough, Amanda heard the door close as he left, heading out to get the wagon. She got up and gathered some diapers and milk before carrying Joyce and her supplies downstairs. All the lights were already on, and everything was ready to go.

For a short while, Amanda walked around the office, carrying Joyce and bouncing her up and down gently in her arms as they went. Eventually, though,

Amanda's arms grew tired, and she placed the baby in her crib behind the counter. Walking over to the window, Amanda moved the curtain to look outside.

A gasp escaped her at what she saw. It seemed like a blizzard was coming in. Large white snowflakes were building up along the ground. They flew through the air with such ferocity that Amanda couldn't see the buildings across the street. *That's not good,* she thought. She instinctively rubbed her upper arms, trying to bring back the warmth. Steven would have to hurry, or else he would get snowed in. With a deep sigh, she walked back towards the counter to sit beside the crib and wait for anyone to arrive.

Within a few hours, the entire world outside that window grew more snowed in and less traversable. Amanda rotated through the different things that Joyce needed. From bottle feedings to burping, diaper changes, and rocking back and forth. She was happy for the chores for the first time, which helped distract her from her worries as the storm blew outside.

She had nearly gotten the baby to sleep when the front door slammed open, wild, white wind bursting in and showering Amanda and the baby with snowflakes. Amanda quickly turned her body, attempting to shield them from the snow. After a moment, the door was pushed shut and the wind died back down. Joyce began to cry as Amanda worked to wipe all the snow off of her.

"How can I help you?" Amanda asked as she turned to see who had arrived. A middle-aged man with a neatly trimmed beard approached the counter. Underneath his dirty, snow-covered jacket, he was holding his left arm very close to his body and he had a deeply pained expression on his face.

"Yes, I need to see Dr. James. I think I have broken my arm," the man said, his voice rising an octave as he spoke.

Amanda swiftly placed Joyce in her crib, even though she was still crying. She grabbed an extra chair and walked it over to the man. "I'm sorry, he had to make a house call. It wasn't supposed to take long, but I think this storm is slowing him down. I'm not sure when he will be back." The man grunted in pain, not seeming too happy about her answer. "What's your name?" she asked him.

He sat down with a frown. "My name's Boris. I'm not sure I'll make it home on my own with this hurt arm and that terrible snowstorm. And it hurts something awful. Is there not anything you can do?" he asked.

Amanda bit the inside of her cheek. "Show it to me." Boris held out his arm slightly, using his other hand to move away the fabric of his shirt and jacket. The lower part of this arm had a broken bone, but the fracture had not broken the skin. However, the bone was protruding wildly, pushing against his skin in a painful-looking manner. In addition, his arm had begun to swell, the skin growing redder and puffier.

Amanda looked up at him. "Are you sure you don't want to wait for Dr. James?"

"It's not about what I want. This pain is too bad to wait any longer," Boris complained, pulling his arm back against his body and cradling it.

Amanda took a deep breath. "If you insist… I must go fetch the medical book to reference what needs to be done. Will you be alright for a moment?"

He nodded with a wince. "As long as you take that crying baby with you." Amanda pursed her lips together and nodded.

Going back behind the counter, she swooped up Joyce and took her down the hall and up the stairs. She bounced her body as she walked, hoping to calm the baby. As she reached the landing, she bounced with Joyce to the kitchen and prepared a new bottle. Then she took her to Steven's room to change her diaper. Once the baby was tended to, Amanda retrieved the book from her room and headed downstairs.

When she got back to the front of the office, she placed the book down on the counter. While still holding Joyce, she began to flip through the pages, going section by section until she got to what she was looking for. Every page of the book showed years of wear, with pencil marks underlining words or circling different parts. Many of the corners of the pages had been folded or roughened down from all the use. Amanda figured that Steven was not the first person to rely on this book.

And now it had come to her.

Reaching the section about fractures, she began to read deeply. As her eyes skimmed over the cumbersome medical words, she couldn't help but notice Boris as he rocked back and forth in his chair from the pain he was experiencing. Thankfully Joyce was calm in her arms.

"Alright, Boris, it looks like we can do a closed reduction of your fracture. That means that we won't cut you open or anything, and hopefully, that will help you start to feel better." Amanda looked up at him to see that he was looking pretty hesitant and wouldn't meet her eye.

"I don't know… are you sure you can do that? It sounds pretty complicated…" He fidgeted in his seat. "Have you ever done anything like this before?"

She sighed with a frown. "Unfortunately, I am still in training, so there are a lot of things that I haven't done. However, if you decide to allow me to do this, I will do the very best that I can. But you are also welcome to wait for Dr. James to return.”

Boris began to glance between her and the arm. Back and forth. Back and forth. His face became more scrunched up with every movement. Finally, he settled on the arm. “Alright, you can fix it. No more waiting.”

Amanda nodded her head. “Let me go get some supplies.”

Still carrying the baby, Amanda walked to the supply closet to get some medicine for pain and a splint. She considered whether or not to move Boris to a patient’s room but decided that moving him now might just cause more problems. After gathering what she needed, Amanda went back to the office and placed Joyce gently in her crib. Thankfully she remained happy, not crying a bit.

"Alright, Boris, take some of this." Amanda handed him a few spoonfuls of the pain medicine. "It will hurt some as I set the bones into place."

He quickly swallowed the medicine and indicated that he was ready with a nod of his head. Amanda brought the splint over to them.

"Place your arm flat against the table, please."

Boris nodded his head and did so. Amanda gently moved the arms of his clothing away from the wound, making sure that nothing was in the way. After it was completely clear, she looked at it for a moment, deciding where the best place to push was. Then, content with what she found, she nodded her head and got her hands ready.

"Are you ready?" she asked. Boris nodded, turning his head to look away.

Carefully, Amanda placed her hands down on the fractured bone before giving it a strong push, popping the bone back into place with an audible sound. Boris gasped and tried pulling away from her, but Amanda held his arm secure and unmoving. Stuck in place under her pressure, Boris began to let loose a string of curse words. As he continued to shout, Amanda grabbed the nearby splint and began to wrap his arm around it. Before he was even done speaking, she had finished securing his newly-set fracture.

He stopped speaking almost instantly to look down at his arm. Amanda removed her hands and gestured to him. After glancing at her, he slowly lifted up his arm, feeling it braced in the splint.

"That wasn't too bad, I guess," he told her, making his face more serious. Amanda gave him a small smile but didn't say anything. Instead, she stood up and began to clean up the supplies. "So, what now?" he asked.

"Well, Dr. James will still need to see it," she said as she stepped closer to the door and peeked out the window. Unfortunately, all she could see was white billowing snow. "If the weather wasn't this bad, I would say you could go home… but I worry about you traveling in this, especially while you are still healing."

Boris frowned and shook his head. "I wish it weren't so, but there is no one waiting for me back at home. I live across town, and I work at the carpenter's shop. Just took a nasty spill while trying to get to the general store."

Amanda nodded. "I recommend that you stay here for the night then, for observation purposes and to make sure that you stay out of this storm."

He glanced around. "Is there anywhere for me to sleep?"

She considered what to do for a moment. "You will come upstairs with us. We have a nice sizable couch by the fire that you can use. That way, I can tend to Joyce and you at the same time."

Boris shrugged in acceptance of her proposal. After gathering the baby and all her supplies, Amanda led Boris up to their home and showed him where he would be sleeping for the night. He fell onto the couch eagerly, though wincing as he went.

Amanda took Joyce into the kitchen with her to start on dinner, and soon she could hear snores coming from the other room.

Chapter Seven

Just outside of town, on a local cattle ranch, Steven paced the foyer of the home. His thudding footsteps echoed throughout the room, but occasionally, when he would pause to look out the window, the sounds of newborn baby coos and people talking gently could be heard. When he had made the drive out here earlier, he had every intention of checking up on the soon-to-be mother Florence and then heading back home. Even as the snowflakes gathered on his coat, he intended on returning home. But when he reached the farmhouse, Florence had just started laboring and she was progressing quickly. Steven had no choice but to stay and help her as she brought a new life into this world.

He was pleased that the timing had worked out so well, but now he was stuck. He had never left Amanda and Joyce alone all night, especially not after leaving them alone all day. His heart clenched, and all kinds of different worries crashed around in his mind.

"Is there anything that I can get you, Doctor?" came a voice, taking him out of his thoughts. He turned to see Florence's mother standing in the doorway, a dish towel hanging off of her arm.

"No, thank you, I'm fine," he said with a nod before turning to look back out of the window at the snowstorm outside.

"Looking at it like that won't make it go away any faster," she told him.

He frowned but did not say anything back or move away from it. Soon he heard her footsteps pad away, leaving him alone again. He wasn't sure what would happen if he did not return tonight, but he was going to find out.

***

Amanda woke up with a startle to cries of pain. Jumping out of bed, she stumbled around for a moment, not sure of where she was or who was hurt. Then, after a moment of thought, she remembered laying down in Steven's bed in order to stay closer to Joyce while Boris stayed with them.

Listening, Amanda quickly realized that Joyce wasn't the one who was crying. However, she had started to fidget, disturbed by the loud noises. Amanda promptly left the room, closing the door behind her.

Stepping into the sitting room, she found Boris tossing and turning in his sleep, seeming to be very confused.

Walking over to him, she spoke firmly but quietly. "Boris, wake up. You're making a lot of noise."

Her words did not stir him. Slowly, she lowered a hand on his shoulder but then pulled it back almost immediately when she realized that his shirt was drenched with sweat. Carefully, she placed her hand on his forehead and found the same thing. He was burning up with a fever.

She quickly walked to the kitchen and got a few rags wet. Then, returning to the couch, she began to dab at his forehead with one of the rags, attempting to cool him and bring down his fever some. It seemed to be helping but only so much.

She retrieved the medicine and had him wake up long enough to drink some. After that, he began to settle down before drifting back off to sleep. Amanda released a sigh of relief before moving towards one of the windows and looking outside. The whole town was covered in fluffs of white that glistened in the moonlight. Not a single footprint littered the snow that led up to their office, not at the front or back.

With a sigh, she walked back to Steven's room, where she sank into his bed, happy that it smelled of him.

***

The snow had finally stopped, and Steven was relieved. Florence's family had been supplying Steven with a nearly endless chain of coffee. He was thankful for them because he knew that otherwise, he would have fallen asleep long ago.

"I'm going to do it," he told Florence's mother, who was sitting with him near the window. "The storm had calmed down. It is the perfect time to return to town."

Florence's mother gave him a wide-eyed look. "You think you will be able to get your wagon through those snowdrifts?"

Steven shrugged. "I think I have to try. I need to return home. I can't leave Amanda alone all night with the baby."

"I'm sure she'll be just fine," Florence's mother informed him.

He nodded in agreement. "You're right, of course. But that doesn't mean that I should make her have to go through that. She did not ask for a baby or even agree to one. I surprised her with it when she arrived. Joyce is not her responsibility."

Florence's mother sighed and shook her head before turning to look at him and pointing her finger aggressively in his direction. "Do not take the wagon. It will get stuck. But just riding the horse…that's a different story. I think you would be able to make it that way. You can leave your wagon here."

Steven's eyes widened and he nodded his head, thinking for a moment. Then all at once, he stood up and took her hand into his, leaning forward to kiss it. "That is a wonderful idea."

With a smile, he let go of her hand and ran to get his bag, getting ready to go out into the landscape of snow.

***

Amanda had only just fallen asleep from helping Boris when Joyce started to cry. Slowly she climbed out of the bed while rubbing her eyes. She felt a spike of irritation growing, but she did her best to ignore it, pushing it down to forget about it. The next few hours progressed similarly. Amanda went between baby and patient, taking care of one then the other.

Boris's fever continued to rise, and she didn't know what to do. He continued to soak through the sheets and shirts she gave him, and no wet rag could keep his forehead cool enough. Finally, she risked a moment to run back downstairs, retrieving the medical book from the counter and hurrying back up. She flipped through the pages as fast as she could, trying to find information on what would help with his fever. Joyce began to cry again. Amanda sighed but got up and gathered the baby into her arms. She slowly walked around Steven's room, trying to settle the girl, when she heard Boris crying out in the other room. Amanda glanced from the baby in her arms to the door, wishing that there was some easy solution. Then, with a firm nod, she carried the baby out and into the other room to attend to both at the same time.

***

After getting his horse saddled up, Steven started out with a promise to return for his wagon once the weather was better. He could also check on the newborn while he was there. The family thanked him again for his help and saw him to the door with well wished.

As soon as he had stepped outside, his breath was nearly taken away by how cold it was. While the air had a solid chill, the wind was ruthless, its ice-cold hands seeping into everything. Climbing onto his horse, he rode out, the horse walking slowly through the tall snowdrifts. As soon as he got out of the shelter of the trees, the drifts were deeper, the snow as high as his horse's knees. It pranced slightly, trying to get its legs farther out with every step. They started on the long journey back into town.

The farther they went, the more Steven wondered if he had made the right decision. Not only had he read about it, but he had seen with his own eyes what the cold weather can do to humans and to animals. The body had ways to fight against it, but only so many. At some point, the cold would become too much, and he would die of hypothermia. But he hoped he would be home far before that was able to occur.

They slowly walked along, making their way through the trail. Most of the familiar landmarks were covered over, but the opening in the treetops showed the road. As they settled into the journey, Steven's thoughts remained on Joyce and Amanda, hoping they were alright. It truly seemed that Amanda was happier lately, and he hoped that he was not simply falling into wishful thinking. Joyce was all of his sister that Steven had left, and he wanted her to be surrounded by joyful and loving people.

But the farther they traveled, the more his thoughts fell to himself. Slowly he counted the things that he could no longer feel. His toes. Fingers. Nose. Ears. What would be next? As the ride drew on, his horse began to protest as well, its steps getting slower as it lost heat and energy.

"Come on, boy, we're almost there," Steven told his horse, hoping that it would believe him. Steven kept his eyes trained ahead of them, straining to see any signs of town. The overcast clouds seemed to be keeping everything just out of sight. He could only guess at how far they had left to travel, as they had never gone this slow before.

Prayers began to filter through his mind as regret began to fill his heart. What if he wasn't even going the right way? What would happen to Amanda and Joyce if he died? No, he mustn't think these things. He would see them again. He would make it back home safe.

And then he saw it. Light. Slowly, through the grey sky, he began to see light emerging, the promise of the town coming slowly within reach. They were almost there.

Almost as if it could sense his excitement, the horse began to pick up the pace, moving faster through the tall snow, heading for town.

Chapter Eight

Joyce was sleeping in Amanda's arms, and Boris was asleep on the couch. Amanda sat on the floor, exhausted and dozing lightly when she heard the sound of the door downstairs and then someone climbing up.

"Who's there?" she called out loudly, attempting to make her voice as aggressive as possible. The creaking paused.

"Amanda… it's me," came a voice.

Her eyes widened. "Steven?" He continued climbing the last stairs and came into view. Amanda sighed with relief and hurried over to him, still holding Joyce and throwing her free arm around him. As she touched him, she immediately drew back with a slight gasp. "You're freezing."

Steven nodded. "It's mighty cold out there. I'm so sorry that it took me so long to return home. I never meant to leave you alone with Joyce for so long. Florence was in labor when I arrived, and so I had to stay—"

"It's alright," Amanda assured him. "But you should know, a man named Boris fell and fractured his arm. He came here looking for you. I ended up doing a closed reduction. He seemed fine, but since then, he has had a terrible fever all night, and I can't get it to go down. He's over here on the couch."

The more she spoke, the more concerned Steven's face became. They quickly walked over to the patient. After Amanda showed Steven what she had been giving Boris, Steven went downstairs to get something else. Slowly, over the next few hours, Steven was able to get the fever down, and Boris was able to sleep much better, finally at peace. By the time that was done, Amanda had been able to get Joyce to bed. In exhaustion and against Steven's recommendation, Amanda had sat down near the couch and had almost immediately fallen asleep.

When Steven was finally done, he looked over at Amanda and smiled. She had refused to leave the room, just in case he needed help and had to wake her. He leaned down and slowly lifted her up into his arms. Then, carefully, he carried her to her bed and tucked her in, kissing her head.

***

Boris was like a new man the next day, finally over his illness and feeling much better. Steven took a look at his arm and determined that everything looked great. Amanda had set the bone well, and there was no need to reset it. Steven had also determined that the fever was unrelated to the break—and for that, he was glad. It seemed the poor man had also caught cold coming through the snow, and that had caused the fever. He sent Boris home with the promise to return in a few weeks to be looked at.

After Boris left, Steven went into Joyce's room, where Amanda had fallen asleep after feeding her. She woke at Steven's touch and looked up at him. Though she was clearly tired after her long night, she also looked proud and happy.

"I did it," she said. "I helped Boris, didn't I? And all while taking care of Joyce."

Steven smiled down at his wife. "You did indeed. I think I may have underestimated your skills. Perhaps I should leave you to handle my patient and tend to Joyce all on your own. I can retire early or take up gardening."

She swatted him playfully on the arm. "Don't you dare leave me alone again! But I must admit, I did enjoy it in a way."

Steven shook his head with a grin. "I think it's time for your training to begin. Would you like to come on a few house calls with me? I think I know a few ladies that would love to look after a sweet baby a few times a week."

"You mean it!" Amanda cried, sitting up quickly and throwing her arms around him. "Oh, yes! Yes, I would."

"Now hand me the big roll of bandages," Amanda said, smiling at the little girl.

Quickly, Joyce ran over to Amanda's big black bag and pulled out the roll of bandages. She brought it over to Amanda and looked at her with wide eyes.

"Will she be all right?" she asked, looking worried.

"Yes," Amanda said. "Now, you hold her leg for me, and then I'll show you how to wrap the bandages around it. Dolly will be as good as new in no time."

Carefully, with a very serious expression, Joyce took hold of her doll's leg just above the pretend break. She watched as Amanda showed her how to place the bandages properly, with not too much or too little tension. Amanda was impressed with Joyce's interest and skills already. Even though she was only four, Joyce already knew the name of all the tools in Amanda and Steven's bags.

After the night of the winter storm, and they called it, Steven had been true to his promise. He had taken Amanda with him on his rounds, and he had quickly discovered that she was indeed a fast learner. After just a few months, he had started letting her diagnose and treat some of his patients at the clinic, which freed him up for more house calls as well as time with Joyce.

Amanda was thrilled, and she took her new responsibilities very seriously. Soon, patients were even coming from neighboring towns to see her, as she was known for her gentle and knowledgeable manner.

"I see we have another patient today."

Joyce and Amanda looked up at the sound of Steven's voice. He held Timothy in his arms as he smiled down at his girls. "This fellow woke up, so I thought I'd bring him into the operating room so he didn't miss all the fun."

"Daddy," Joyce pouted, looking up from applying a bit of iodine to her doll's head, "this is not fun. Doctoring is serious."

Amanda and Steven exchanged grins as Steven set two-year-old Timothy down next to Joyce. Immediately, the little girl began showing her brother how to apply another bandage to the poor dolly.

"She's right, you know," Steven said, looking at Amanda with love. "Doctoring is serious. It has to be something you love."

Amanda smiled back at him. "And it's even better with someone you love."

The End

Just to say thanks for checking our works we like to gift you

Our Exclusive Never Before Released Books

100% FREE!

Please GO TO

http://cleanromancepublishing.com/gift

And get your FREE gift

Thanks for being such a wonderful client.

Please Check out My Other Works

By checking out the link below

http://cleanromancepublishing.com/fjauth

Many thanks for taking the time to buy and read through this book.

It means lots to be supported by SPECIAL **readers like** YOU**.**

Hope you enjoyed the book; please support my writing by leaving an honest review to assist other readers.

.

With Regards,

Faith Johnson